A KINDLE OF KIT

Rumer Godden

Illustrated by Lynne Byrnes

For Seamus

Text © Rumer Godden 1978
Illustrations © Lynne Byrnes 1978

First published 1978 by
Macmillan London Limited
London and Basingstoke
All rights reserved
ISBN 0 333 32964 3

Picturemac edition published 1982
Reprinted 1983

Printed in Hong Kong

She was a little tabby cat, striped on her legs and tail, and with a small striped face in which her eyes looked as big as half-pence. No one knew how she came to live in the town and she did not know either; she did not belong to anyone, but sometimes in the early morning—so early that the sun was not up—she would walk along the tiles of the highest roof in the town and sit on the ridgepole looking down on all the other roofs with their chimney pots; then the town belonged to her.

She sat on the ridgepole washing herself, one leg stuck up in the air, until the clouds turned pink.

She had no name so that the townspeople called her Cat. The kindly ones put out scraps for her, even saucers of milk; the unkind ones said "Shoo!" and often threw shoes or slippers at her. Cat did not mind; there were plenty of alleys and passage-ways in this old town down which a little cat could vanish. She ran along the tops of high garden walls and slept where she liked—under a car, even on the bonnet of a car if it were warm, or in a wheelbarrow or an outhouse if someone left the door open.

She never went into a real house but she knew all their dustbins.

The town was so old that it still had its "big house", the Mansion House, where an important lady and gentleman lived; by the size of the meat-bones and fish-spines and the number of wine bottles in their dustbins Cat knew they were important and had many guests.

There was a Town Crier, too, who put on a purple caped coat and a cocked hat and went round the cobbled streets ringing his bell and crying "Oyez! Oyez!" to tell the town news; he much amused the visitors. He also had a well-filled dustbin and his wife gave Cat some of her best scraps.

There was a rude boy who crossed his fingers and spat when he saw Cat because he believed cats, unless they were black, were unlucky; sometimes he threw, not shoes but stones at her. The Quiet Woman suffered from him too; she was called the Quiet Woman because she kept her curtains drawn and, if she had to go out shopping, slipped out of her house with her basket when no one was about and, as quickly as possible, slipped back again. She seldom spoke to anyone and there was little in her dustbin because she gave almost everything away, not to people but to the birds or a stray dog; to Cat as well.

And there was the Poet. "*My wishful fishful sprite*," he said when
he saw Cat. She wished she were fishful! The Poet had no dustbin
at all; like Cat he lived on what people gave him because, unlike
her, he often forgot about food. He walked around the town talking
to himself. No wonder. He had wonderful words.

> "*Out of doors I see the spring*
> *Creeping through the alleys dim*,"

chanted the Poet,

> "*For I see the young moon's ring . . .*"

Like the Poet, Cat often walked the streets but she walked mostly at night along the empty pavements, waving her tail; and she, too, liked the moon, but best when it was full. Then she would go up on the ridgepole and look at the town silvered with moonlight.

One warm night she heard a miaoul; it was a soft crooning miaoul, more entrancing than any noise she had ever heard. It was made by a big dark cat with a handsome white vest. He came and sat beside her on the ridgepole.

"Tell me your name."

"Cat," said Cat.

"I am He-Cat."

"Then . . . I am She-Cat," Cat said shyly.

"Queen Cat," and he came closer.

"King Cat," said She-Cat.

Then they did not sit on the ridgepole any longer; he chased her and the miaouls became caterwauls.

Some weeks later She-Cat began to feel fat. *The fat cat sat on the mat*, says the old spelling book; it would have been wiser to sit on the mat. She-Cat began to find it difficult to climb up to the ridgepole.

"I am going to have kittens," said She-Cat to herself. "Here's a nice kindle!"

The kindly people said, "Kittens! Poor little thing! We must send for the Animal Welfare Man. He will take them away."

The people who said "Shoo!" said the same thing, but not kindly. "Disgraceful! More stray cats! Telephone the Welfare Man at once."

"Kittens!" said the rude boy. "Drown them in a bucket."

She-Cat clambered slowly up to the ridgepole and washed, but she could no longer put a leg up in the air; the stripes on her face looked like furrows and her eyes were as big as one-pence pieces. 'I wish I knew how many kits,' she thought. 'Some queens have three'—the Poet had told her "queen" was the proper name for a she-cat. 'Some queens have only two, but some have four or five or *six*.' At the thought of six, her fur seemed to stand on end—but she had only four.

One was dark like He-Cat: one was marmalade: one was fluffy and handsome: the last, a little queen, was tabby like She-Cat, but they all had white vests.

They were born in a broken greenhouse among flower-pots, empty sacks and a rubbish heap, all belonging to a deaf old man who never went into his garden.

At first it was delightful; the kittens were like warm little bags of fur; all they could do was suck and sleep and purr. She-Cat had never heard purring before; she began to purr too.

The dark kitten had a face that, when he purred or cried, went into comical wrinkles, and so she called him Funny. The marmalade kitten's orange fur was so like sun-rays that she called him Sunny. The fluffy one was so handsome and elegant she was sure he was valuable and so she called him Money. The tiny tabby was so sweet that She-Cat called her Honey.

But presently the kittens opened their eyes and grew.

They grew so quickly that soon they were staggering over the greenhouse floor and climbing up flower-pots and falling into them. They were so hungry that She-Cat's milk was not enough and she had to carry them scraps—*her* scraps. They made so much noise that she was sure even the deaf old man would find them. She seemed to hear shouts of "Animal Welfare Man," and "Buckets."

She-Cat climbed up to the ridgepole—it was easy as she was thin again, too thin; her eyes now looked as big as two-pences. She sat on the ridgepole and thought.

She was too worried to wash.

'It's all very well for me,' thought She-Cat, 'to walk on the pavements at night, sleep on the bonnets of cars or in a wheelbarrow; to eat what people give me or what I can find in dustbins, but for my kittens. . .'

She imagined four kittens scampering everywhere after her, falling off garden walls, getting under cars, climbing into dustbins, and she shut her eyes in horror.

Then she opened her eyes and looked down over the roofs of the houses of the town. "They must each live in one of those houses," said She-Cat. "I must choose."

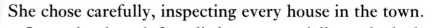

She chose carefully, inspecting every house in the town.

It was hard work for a little cat, especially as she had to go back to the greenhouse every two hours to give the kittens her milk, but she went round and round until the pads of her paws were sore; round and round, looking up at people's faces to see if they were likely to telephone the Welfare Man or had rude boys with buckets. She also looked at all the dustbins.

At last she made her choice.

Funny was to go to the Town Crier. His voice was louder than the Crier's, even louder than the bell, and if visitors were amused at the Town Crier, they would be amused at Funny, even if he hadn't a cocked hat; besides, the Town Crier's wife was generous and their dustbin excellent.

It was quite easy; She-Cat had only to put Funny in the Town Crier's way, so she took Funny in her mouth and carried him by the scruff of his neck and laid him on the pavement at the Town Crier's feet just as the Town Crier was shouting "Oyez! Oyez!"

Then she went behind a doorpost to watch.

Funny let out a mew so loud that the Town Crier stopped. He picked Funny up.

"Lost cat! Lost cat! Oyez!" cried the Town Crier. "Oyez! Anybody lost a kitten? Oyez!"

There was naturally no answer, so the Town Crier took Funny home to his wife, and that is where Funny has been ever since.

The Quiet Woman was to have Sunny. 'She needs a little sun in those dark rooms,' She-Cat had thought. Again it was easy; she knew she had only to mew and rub herself against the door and the Quiet Woman would open it.

She-Cat carried Sunny as she had carried Funny and put Sunny on the doorstep, rubbed at the door and mewed, and ran away and hid.

As the Quiet Woman came out, a sun ray caught Sunny's coat so that it glowed with such marmalade colours that the Quiet Woman blinked; then she gave a little gasp.

She lifted Sunny up and cradled him in her hands. Sunny put out his rough little tongue to give the Quiet Woman a shy lick on her chin where, to She-Cat's astonishment, tears were running down.

She-Cat could hear Sunny purring as the Quiet Woman carried him in.

She was never as quiet again; her curtains were pulled back and often she could be seen standing on her doorstep holding Sunny and talking to all the people who admired him.

Money was more difficult because She-Cat had decided that, for such a handsome and elegant kitten, the only fitting house was the Mansion House. 'Its lady has dimples,' thought She-Cat, 'and ladies with dimples are usually kind. The gentleman has a beard and beards are rather frightening, but his eyes are gentle and so is his voice.' Money, she was sure, would never see the dustbins; a pity when they were so good. But how to get into the Mansion House? Its front door was not opened unless somebody knocked or rang and how could a small cat do either? At the back door there was a DOG.

She-Cat discovered that the Mansion House was open to the public on Wednesday afternoons. 'Well, I am part of the public,' thought She-Cat, 'so it is open to me.' It seemed visitors could go into the drawing-rooms and the garden but were not allowed upstairs, but, 'That's where I shall have to go,' thought She-Cat.

Next Wednesday afternoon she took Money in her mouth; he was the heaviest of the kittens and she could not help his bumping on the pavement. Stone steps led up to the Mansion House front door, and she waited with Money in their shadow until a party of visitors came and the front door was opened. She slipped in among them—there were so many legs she and Money were not noticed. While the visitors bought their tickets, she took Money upstairs; limp as a stuffed sock he bumped on every step but he could not cry as his scruff was in her mouth.

There was no sign of the lady or gentleman, but their bedroom door was open and She-Cat saw a big bed with a lace and satin cover. She jumped up on it—that was an effort with such a big kitten in her mouth—and laid Money against a cushion that was covered in lace and satin too. Money suited it and it suited Money; he purred and fell asleep against it—perhaps he was tired from the bumping.

She-Cat thought, when she left him, that Money had never looked as handsome; the lady and gentleman must have thought so too because Money became the Mansion House cat.

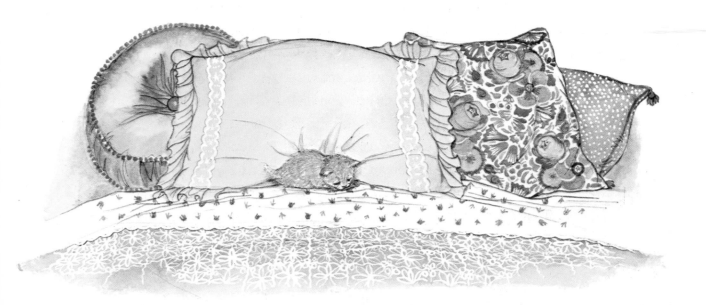

That left Honey. 'Dare I,' thought She-Cat, 'dare I trust the Poet with Honey? He is the nicest man in the town but he has no dustbin, and he does use such a number of words and he does do all that walking. Still,' she thought, 'Honey will have as much to eat with him as with me, probably more because the Poet is popular.' Indeed someone had just given him a whole turkey; She-Cat knew that because she had found the bones in his back garden. Honey was used to a tumble of mews and miaows and purrs so she would not mind his words, and as for walking, she was so small the Poet could put her in his pocket.

Honey had never looked as small as when she was put on the Poet's doorstep, but She-Cat should not have feared; she had miaowed outside the door and the Poet came out and looked round for her, then looked down and saw the kitten. Honey looked up at him, opened her tiny mouth to mew . . . but there was no need.

"*Oh my small, my sweet, my fine, my fair*
  My darling . . ." cried the Poet.

He picked Honey tenderly up and put her where She-Cat had hoped she would be, in his pocket.

Later that afternoon, she saw him coming out of the dairy with a bottle of milk; next he went into the fishmonger's.

She-Cat did not go back to the greenhouse; it was too empty. She went up to the ridgepole and sat there all night, but she knew her kittens were happy and settled in life.

Towards midnight Cat heard a soft entrancing crooning miaoul and saw a dark shape with a white vest, but she shut her ears and her eyes tight.

Towards morning she started to wash; she could stick one leg high up into the air now.

She washed and washed until the clouds grew pink.

The Poet's words are taken from poems by Fredegond Shove, and I must also make grateful acknowledgement to Patrick S. Collier who gave me, among other things, the collective noun of the title and taught me that "to kindle" can mean "to give birth".